Sled Run for Survival

FOCUS ON THE FAMILY PRESENTS

Sled Run for Survival

BOOK 29

MARIANNE HERING
ILLUSTRATIONS BY SERGIO CARIELLO

FOCUS
ON THE FAMILY.

A Focus on the Family Resource
Published by Tyndale House Publishers

To Karen B., who helped me through
a difficult journey.

—M.H.

Sled Run for Survival
© 2022 Focus on the Family. All rights reserved.

A Focus on the Family book published by Tyndale House Publishers, Carol Stream, Illinois 60188

Focus on the Family, The Imagination Station, Adventures in Odyssey, and their accompanying logos and designs, are federally registered trademarks of Focus on the Family, 8605 Explorer Drive, Colorado Springs, CO 80920.

Tyndale and Tyndale's quill logo are registered trademarks of Tyndale House Ministries.

Scripture quotations marked (NIrV) are taken from the Holy Bible, *New International Reader's Version*®, *NIrV.*® Copyright © 1995, 1996, 1998, 2014 by Biblica, Inc.® Used by permission. All rights reserved worldwide. (*www.zondervan.com*) The "NIrV" and "New International Reader's Version" are trademarks registered in the United States Patent and Trademark Office by Biblica, Inc.®

With the exception of known historical figures, all characters are the product of the authors' imaginations.

Cover art and interior illustrations by Sergio Cariello. Additional spot illustrations from Vectorstock.

For Library of Congress Cataloging-in-Publication Data for this title, visit http://www.loc.gov/help/contact-general.html.

For manufacturing information regarding this product, please call 1-855-277-9400.

For information about special discounts for bulk purchases, please contact Tyndale House Publishers at csresponse@tyndale.com, or call 1-855-277-9400.

ISBN 978-1-64607-015-2

Printed in the United States of America

28 27 26 25 24 23 22
7   6   5   4   3   2   1

Contents

Snowbound

Beth followed her cousin Patrick down the
steps to the workshop at Whit's End.

Patrick pushed open the basement door.
The cousins burst inside.

"It's a snow day!" Patrick shouted.

"No school till next week," Beth added.

They took off their jackets and hung them
on a coatrack.

Beth slipped off her yellow rubber boots and

1

left them near the door. She padded across the floor in her socks. She stopped next to Whit.

The inventor put his wrench down on his workbench. His skin looked chapped, and he had frost in his eyebrows. He smiled at the cousins.

"Were you shoveling snow?" Patrick asked.

Whit shook his head. "I was just testing out an Imagination Station adventure in—"

"Don't tell me," Beth said. "The Sahara Desert?"

Whit laughed at her joke. His eyes twinkled. "Somewhere much colder," he said.

Whit plucked a white hair off his black wool sweater.

"Fighting a polar bear?" Patrick asked. He made motions as if jabbing a bear with a long stick. "They're the biggest bears on the planet."

Whit was silent for a moment. He shook his

head again. "I was fighting something much more dangerous," he said.

"A wolf then?" Patrick said.

"No," Whit said.

"Walruses," Patrick said. "They have long tusks." He pointed his index fingers downward. Then he pressed them against his puckered lips.

Beth giggled at Patrick's finger tusks.

"Walruses are strong," Whit said. "But this was a fiercer opponent than all the wild animals combined."

Beth wondered what it could be.

Whit picked up something from the workbench. "Why don't you test out the adventure for me," he said. "I think you'll find this one a challenge."

Whit walked to the Imagination Station. It looked like the cockpit of a helicopter. But there were no spinning blades on top.

He opened the control panel on the side. He fiddled with some buttons, and the machine's door slid open.

Patrick motioned for Beth to get in first. She slid into the far seat. She ran her hand across the dials on the dashboard.

Patrick followed, settling into the black leather seat. He put on his seatbelt.

Beth fastened hers, too.

Whit held up a pair of old-fashioned earmuffs. They had puffy wool pads to cover a person's ears. "This is a new version of the translation device," he said. "Who had it last time?"

Patrick pointed at Beth. "She got to talk to dolphins with a conch shell," he said.

Beth thought Patrick sounded a little jealous.

Whit handed the earmuffs to Patrick. "You'll need these," he said. "Communication is important on this adventure."

Patrick took the earmuffs and set them on his lap.

"Will I be able to speak 'girl talk'?" Patrick asked. He elbowed Beth gently.

"Hardy har har," Beth said.

Beth saw some little orange packets on the floor of the Imagination Station. She knew they were Hot Handz hand warmers.

"You'll need those," Whit said, nodding at the packets. "Keep them with you."

Beth picked up the packets. She was about to ask what else besides good communication would be needed.

But before she could ask, Patrick hit the red button. The machine lurched.

Beth felt as if she were on a sled, sliding down an icy hill. Then she felt the machine spin in circles. She felt dizzy and excited all at once.

Then everything went black.

The Ice

Patrick got out of the Imagination Station. He stood in a large, snow-covered open space. Trees encircled the area.

All he could see in every direction was the white and gray of winter. The world seemed to be one enormous snow globe. Snow frosted the trees and nearby shrubs. Distant rocks looked like giant marshmallows. Round, white clouds with gray bellies floated across the sky.

He breathed out, and his breath formed mini clouds.

Patrick glanced at the Imagination Station. Beth was climbing out of it. She was dressed in animal pelts. A large, furry backpack clung to her back.

Beth stepped away from the Imagination Station. The machine seemed to melt into the hilly landscape and disappear.

A chill traveled up Patrick's sleeve. They would need those Hot Handz.

Patrick looked at his clothes. The machine had transformed him into a human bundle of fur. Like Beth, he was wearing a jacket, pants, and boots made from animal pelts. He touched his arm and saw he was wearing thick mittens made from black fur. Beaver skin?

He took off a mitten and felt his head. He had on a fuzzy hood with fur trim. The translation device was covering his ears. The earmuffs felt warm. He listened carefully, hoping to hear a bird or something.

But the only things he heard were wind and an odd whistling sound. A sudden gust swooshed across the flat land. It picked up a mini cyclone of snow, pushing it toward him.

Beth moved away from the swirling snow. She stepped into a thick grove of spruce.

The sound of an engine came from above. Patrick looked up.

A yellow biplane was over the trees. The pilot waved as the plane passed overhead. The cousins could see that the pilot was wearing thick goggles and a yellow scarf.

"Hey!" Beth shouted. "Here! Down here!"

Patrick jumped and shouted, "We need a ride!"

But the plane flew away toward the west.

As he jumped, Patrick heard a *crack* below him. The ground moaned and made eerie popping sounds.

He looked down. He was not standing on land but on snow-covered ice. And the ice was splitting. His heart raced.

Beth watched the crack between Patrick's feet widen.

"Jump toward me!" she shouted. "Or you'll fall in!"

Patrick pushed off of one leg. He crossed over the crack and dove on his stomach, sliding a few feet.

Beth rushed down the small slope. She stopped at the edge of the ice.

"Now pull yourself toward me!" she said. "You're six feet away from safety."

Patrick moved his arms and legs. He wriggled forward slowly. Just as he got near the edge, the gap widened. It was about eighteen inches wide now.

Her heart was pounding. *What if Patrick falls in? What if he drags me into the water with him? We'll both freeze to death within minutes.*

But Beth took a deep breath. She leaned forward and took hold of his wrists. She pulled him off the ice.

"Thanks," Patrick said. "That was a close call. Weren't you afraid I would pull you into the water?"

Beth nodded and gave a weak smile. "I'm glad we're both okay."

The cousins stood up and brushed off the powdery snow.

"Listen," Beth said. "The ice is singing."

The frozen lake moaned and popped and crackled.

"Weird," Patrick said. "I've never heard that before."

The sounds grew deeper in tone.

"It sounds angry now," Patrick said. "Let's go."

"Which way?" Beth asked. "Mr. Whittaker didn't say much. We're looking for something dangerous."

"Like that?" Patrick asked. He pointed behind her.

Beth turned around.

A moose was crashing through the spruce trees.

Beth froze. It was the strangest animal she had ever seen. It had only one antler. But that wasn't all. A white wolf had taken hold of the moose's front leg. It was not going to let go.

The moose let out another deep moan. Patrick lifted his mitten to the earmuffs.

"The translation device is working!" he shouted. "I can understand the moose—sort of."

"Let me guess," she said. "It's afraid."

"How did you know?" Patrick asked.

Beth smiled. "We should find some cover," she said. Then she turned and moved behind a large spruce.

Patrick followed. But his boots sank into the deep snow. He had to lift each leg high to take the next step.

The moose moved straight into the spruce grove. It dragged the wolf with it. The moose thrashed its head wildly as if trying to bite the wolf.

But the white animal's teeth held on to the loose skin at the top of the moose's leg.

The moose moaned and thrashed again. Its antler banged into a tree trunk.

The moose walked on, dragging the wolf into a small clearing.

"Look," Beth said, "the moose's antler fell off."

Patrick remembered the translation device. He shouted to the moose, "Hey, Mr. Moose, brush the wolf against the tree! It will let go!"

But the moose kept walking and groaning.

The moose stepped toward a large pine that was missing branches. It pinned the wolf against the tree and leaned.

"It listened to me, Beth! It listened to me!"

The wolf let go of the moose. But then it turned toward the cousins and snarled. Patrick saw its long, sharp teeth. Moose blood dripped from its mouth.

"Okay, Dr. Dolittle," Beth said. "Please tell the wolf to leave us alone."

Patrick shouted at the white creature, "Go home!"

The wolf stepped closer, the silvery gray tips of its ears twitching.

"This is its home," Beth said. "We're the newcomers."

Patrick reacted quickly. He picked up the fallen antler and held the pointed side outward. "Get behind me!" he said.

The Wolf King

Beth crouched near Patrick. She heard a far-off jingling sound coming from behind her. She wondered if that was the bell at Whit's End.

She looked around for the Imagination Station to rescue them, but she didn't see it anywhere. She didn't hear the machine's familiar hum either.

But the jingles grew closer . . . as did the white wolf.

Beth could now see its left ear was ragged and scarred. A silver streak ran from its forehead to its nose. Its almond-shaped eyes were close-set and glowed like yellow jewels.

Patrick thrust the antler in the wolf's direction. "Yah! Get back!" he shouted.

"Tell the wolf we don't taste good," Beth said. "Human meat might upset its stomach."

The wolf snarled.

"*His* stomach," Patrick said. "He said he's the alpha male."

Patrick said in a kind voice, "Hi, wolf king. Let's talk this through . . ."

Excited yips and high-pitched howls mixed with the jingles coming from behind them.

The hair along the wolf's back rose and formed a spiky ridge of menace.

Beth didn't dare take her eyes off the white wolf king.

"Listen! More wolves are coming," Beth said, putting a hand on Patrick's back. "This must be the danger that Whit meant."

"Not wolves," Patrick said. "I hear dogs through the translation device. Happy dogs."

Patrick turned and looked behind him.

Just then, the wolf sprang.

Beth screamed as the wolf lunged. The animal's teeth bit into the backpack.

Patrick swung the antler and knocked the white wolf away. The wolf hit the snow on his side but quickly bounced back to his feet.

Suddenly a gunshot rang out. The sound echoed off the snowy hills.

The wolf let go of the backpack. But his fur was still raised, and his teeth were bared in a snarl. He had retreated only about six feet.

The jingling and yapping were closer now. A sled pulled by seven large dogs drove into the small clearing.

The dogs were large and of differing colors. They had bells on their harnesses.

A man stood on the sled. Its cargo was several large, white canvas bags. The musher wore a fur jacket with a hood that covered most of his face. But Patrick could see he was old with a thick, white beard.

Patrick thought the man might have looked

like Father Christmas except for one thing: the rifle in his hands.

"The wolf," said Beth to the musher. "Please—he's after us."

The musher sprang off the sled and rushed at the wolf. He held the rifle like a club. "Go on, get out of here!" he shouted and waved the weapon.

The sled dogs yelped and yipped as if to encourage their master. The bells on their harnesses shook and jingled loudly.

The wolf king backed away.

Patrick could understand the hunger in his growl. He wanted food for himself and his pack.

Then the wolf ran off, nose to the snow, sniffing. Patrick knew he was following the scent of the moose.

The musher lowered his weapon. "Phillip Clearsky at your service," he said.

Beth walked over to him and shook his hand, thick mitten to thick mitten. She said,

"I'm Beth." She motioned toward Patrick. "And this is my cousin Patrick."

Patrick also shook Clearsky's hand.

"Thank you for firing your rifle to scare the wolf away," Patrick said.

"Oh, I wasn't trying to scare the wolf," he said. "I didn't even see it at first."

"Then why did you fire the rifle?" Beth asked. "The shot came at the perfect time."

"A crazed moose came running at my sled," Clearsky said. "I was afraid it would kick one of my dogs. So I fired a warning shot, and it ran away."

"Anyway, it helped us scare the wolf," Beth said. "Thank you."

"You two have an odd accent," he said. "It reminds me of a visitor we had a few days ago. You ever met a man named Whittaker?"

The cousins nodded.

"Mr. Whittaker sort of dropped us off here," Patrick said.

"He is an odd one. Though nice enough," Clearsky said. "I'm glad he gave up on that silly idea of his."

Patrick looked at Beth. They both shrugged. Neither seemed to know what Whit's silly idea was.

The dogs began to whine and yelp. They wanted to get going so they could eat.

The musher pointed to the sun hanging low in the sky. "Not much daylight in January. I've got to hurry," he said. "I don't want to travel in the dark."

Patrick glanced at the bags on the sled. They all had *U.S. Mail* printed on the side. *We're in the United States with snow and mountains and sled dogs*, he thought. *Alaska?*

"May we have a ride into town?" Beth asked. "We got a little farther out than we realized."

"Sure. You two look light enough," Clearsky said. "Hop on, and I'll take you to Nome."

Beth threw her backpack on top of the mailbags. Then she climbed on top of the sled. Patrick stood on the musher's footboards.

Finally, Clearsky bent to pet his dogs. He scratched the lead dog behind the ears. "Good girl, Storm," he said. Then he got on the back of the sled and shouted, "Hike!"

The dogs began to run.

Patrick felt a gentle breeze. He listened to the harness bells as the sled slid along packed snow. The single dog in front, Storm, yapped and barked.

Using the translation device, Patrick knew the dog was just happy—she was made for this work. She was saying, "Hurry, hurry," to the dogs tethered behind her in pairs.

In the distance came a wailing howl. Patrick wondered if the sound meant the wolf had caught the moose.

Danger in Nome

The dogsled slid west. Beth noticed the landscape changed with every mile. The snow felt firmer and icier. The trees thinned till there were none. The land became more level.

Beth observed the musher and learned the "language" of dogsledding. He shouted "Gee!" to tell the lead dog to go right. "Haw!" meant left. "Easy" meant to go slowly.

Finally, Beth saw a town up ahead. A

banner across the sled trail said "Welcome to Nome, Alaska Territory."

A large, ice-covered sea was just to the west. Farther up the shore stood machinery and warehouses.

The buildings in town reminded Beth of an old Western movie set. Snow covered the ground, but the wood walkways in front of the shops and other buildings had been cleared. One was a church with a tall steeple.

Clearsky stepped off the sled. He told the dogs to "line out." The animals moved so that the harness was tight, and they weren't getting tangled.

Patrick stepped off and grabbed one of the mailbags. "Where does this go?" he asked Clearsky.

The old musher pointed to a white building with the words *Post Office* written on a sign over the door.

"Thanks, Patrick," Clearsky said. "I'll see to the dogs while you unload. A good musher always sees to his dogs first."

Beth could now see Phillip Clearsky's face close up. He had a broad, pleasant face. His eyes were crinkled with smile lines.

He bent over to unhitch Storm from the harness, and she licked his face. Soon all the dogs had been unharnessed. They began to nip one another and wrestle playfully.

The dogs followed Clearsky to a shack-like house.

Beth went inside with them. The room was filled with wooden boxes about two and a half feet square.

Clearsky lit a small stove in the corner. Then he took a large pan outside and filled it with snow. He melted the snow and poured the water into a pail. The dogs scrambled to drink first.

Beth helped by taking the pan outside and filling it with more snow.

"This is an odd building," Beth said as she came back inside. "It's so small, and the roof is so low. It seems almost like a playhouse."

"It's an old miner's cabin," he said. "They were built small to keep the heating costs low."

"So Nome was a mining town?" she asked.

"Yep," Clearsky said. "People from the States, Russia, and Europe started coming here in 1899 to look for gold."

Beth said, "That's, uh . . ." Then she paused and looked at him. "I'm having trouble with the math—that's how many years ago?" she asked.

"Twenty-six," Clearsky said.

Beth considered the year 1925. World War I had recently ended. World War II wouldn't start for several years.

What is the danger about this place? she

wondered. *It's unlikely that an enemy would attack.*

"I'm going to get some food for the dogs," Clearsky said.

Beth took off a mitten and petted the dogs while he was gone. Their fur was soft and thick.

Clearsky came back with a burlap sack and a large pail. He turned the sack over, and lumps of dried salmon fell out.

"What is that?" Beth said, pointing at the pail. It was filled with weird pink meat that still had skin on it.

"Whale fat," Clearsky said. "These dogs need lots of calories."

He tossed a piece of the fat and some of the salmon into each of the boxes.

"We're all done here," Clearsky said. He stepped outside. Beth followed him. "I'm going to collect the outgoing mail. Then I'll head to my next stop."

Clearsky waved goodbye and headed toward a row of nearby buildings.

Beth stood and stared at the frozen sea. A gentle fog was rolling in. It formed a mist over the ice. Everything seemed so quiet and peaceful. She wondered, *Where is the danger?*

Patrick hurried toward Beth. He was carrying the backpack.

"Let's look inside this now," he said. He set the pack on a bench outside City Hall.

"Good idea," she said.

Beth inspected the pack. Teeth marks from the wolf had made a few small tears.

She pulled open the drawstring and looked inside. She held up a lump of something wrapped in white paper. The words *Beef Jerky* were written on the side.

"No wonder that wolf wanted the backpack," she said.

"What else is there?" Patrick asked.

Beth pulled out a metal whistle and a box of rock salt.

"Mr. Whittaker uses this," Patrick said, pointing to the salt. "He sprinkles it on the sidewalks in snowy weather. It keeps the snow from forming ice."

"I've churned homemade ice cream and used rock salt," Beth said. "It keeps the water from freezing. But it stays cold enough to make ice cream."

Beth blew on the whistle. It didn't make any sound. "This seems to be broken," she said.

Then she put the items back inside the pack. "I guess we'll know when the time comes to use these things." Then she took the Hot Handz out of her pockets and handed a few to Patrick.

Patrick slid the foil packets inside an inner coat pocket.

Beth put the rest of the packets inside the backpack and pulled the drawstring closed.

"Do you think the danger Whit mentioned is the weather?" Beth said.

"Maybe . . ." Patrick said.

Just then six men came out of a two-story building. Patrick could just read the sign over the entrance: *Hospital*.

The men rushed away from the building. Two of them hurried toward the bench. A biting wind came with them. Their animal-skin boots crushed the icy snow with each step. Their heads were down so Patrick couldn't see their faces.

"Patrick!" one of them shouted to be heard over the wind. It was Phillip Clearsky. "I need your help!"

"What is it?" Patrick asked.

"I need someone to come with me to the Sandpit," Clearsky said. He gestured with his arms toward the sled. "We need to tell the Eskimos who live there to stay inside their igloos. The Nome town council just met. It's official: We've got an outbreak."

"An outbreak of the Spanish flu?" asked Beth.

"Worse," the other man said. "Diphtheria.

It's called 'The Strangler' because it causes children to choke to death."

Patrick gulped. He looked at Beth.

"That *is* more dangerous than wild animals," she whispered.

Quarantine

"I'll harness the dogs," Clearsky said.

"Can I gather them?" Patrick asked the musher. He nodded, and Patrick shouted, "Storm! Bring the team!"

The dogs dashed out of the shed, yipping and wagging their tails.

Clearsky looked at Beth. "It'll be faster with just Patrick and me."

Beth felt a twinge of jealousy. But it passed

quickly. She smiled and wished them a safe trip.

Clearsky and Patrick headed toward the doghouse.

Beth was alone with the unknown man. She looked at him and said, "I'm Beth."

"Hello, young lady," the man said. "I'm the county doctor, Dr. Welch. I need you to go home. Talk to no one. If you see someone coming near, shout, 'Stay away. The town is on quarantine.' "

Beth knew all about quarantines. Not long ago her school had been shut down because of a virus.

She also knew that she'd been vaccinated against diphtheria. But how could she tell Dr. Welch without lying? Vaccines to prevent diphtheria hadn't been invented in 1925. She didn't want to explain the Imagination Station. He wouldn't believe her.

"I can help. I can warn the townspeople," Beth said. She chose her next words carefully. "My home doctor is ahead of the times. He gave me shots to keep me from getting diphtheria. I'm immune."

"Is that so?" Dr. Welch said. "I've got to keep up with the medical journals then. Right now, I don't have time for a vaccine. I need antitoxin. It's too late to prevent the spread. I need to kill all the bacteria. Many young children will die unless they get the antitoxin."

The doctor looked Beth in the eyes. "You don't live around here. You'll need a guide to show you around."

Beth nodded.

"See that small, white house up that hill?" the doctor asked. He pointed to another building. It was the same size as the one for the dogs.

She nodded again.

Dr. Welch said, "A boy named Joe Walsh will be in there. Tell him what I told you. He knows all the people in town. The two of you can quickly reach a lot of people. And give me a report when you get back."

"Yes, sir," Beth said.

The doctor gave her a few more instructions. Then she turned and headed to the small house.

She knocked on the door.

A boy's voice answered, "Come in and shut the door quickly."

Beth entered and pulled the door closed. The house had been stripped to make a barn. Two kerosene lamps hanging on wall hooks lit the room. A gray dog lay curled up in a straw bed.

Two cows stood in small stalls. Bales of hay were stacked in the back of the building. Each animal had a thick quilt strapped to its back. The cows mooed softly when Beth approached.

A redheaded boy about eleven years old sat on a wooden stool milking a cow. Beth figured he was Joe Walsh. The boy's hands worked skillfully on the cow's udder. Milk squirted into a large metal can.

"Hi," she said. "I'm Beth. I don't mean to be pushy, but you have to come with me. Dr. Welch needs you to show me around town. The people need to quarantine. There's a diphtheria outbreak."

Joe looked up without slowing down the milking process. He said, "That must be what little Billy Barnett died of. He was in the hospital for two weeks. We prayed for him last Sunday at church." Then he looked back at the cow and kept milking.

"I'm sorry," Beth said. "His parents and friends must be sad."

Joe nodded and kept milking the cow. The milk was still squirting out in a strong flow.

What part of "diphtheria outbreak" is difficult to understand? Beth wondered. *He'll be milking that cow forever.*

"Well?" Beth said aloud. "Are we going or not?"

"I'm going as fast as I can," Joe said. "I can't leave ol' Belle when she needs to be milked. Her udder could get infected."

"Oh," Beth said. "Sorry. Can I help?"

"Sure," Joe said. "Grab a bucket and stool. You can milk Clara."

Beth moved a stool to Clara's side. She put a pail underneath the cow.

She grabbed the cow's udder and squeezed.

A spray of milk went right into her face. She licked some drops that dribbled down to her lips. The liquid was sweet, warm, and creamy.

Joe laughed.

Beth got the next few squirts in the bucket.

Then Clara lifted her back hoof and kicked the pail. It fell over, spilling the milk into the straw. Belle mooed, and it sounded like a cow laugh to Beth.

Beth's cheeks flushed red with embarrassment.

Joe said, "I'll finish up the milking." Then he nodded toward the sleeping gray dog. "Take Turk and harness him to the sled. It's around back."

Beth was glad to be given an easier task. She called Turk.

The dog lifted his head and looked at Joe.

"It's okay, boy," Joe said. "I'll be there in a minute."

After those words, Turk followed Beth out and walked dutifully to the sled.

Beth bent and picked up leather straps that lay on the sled. She eyed the straps and buckles of the gang line. Then she fastened them around Turk's furry chest and neck.

Joe came out of the shed carrying the metal

milk tote and two kerosene lamps. He placed the lidded tote on the sled. Beth put her backpack next to them.

"Hike," he said to Turk.

The dog yipped and pulled the sled with the milk can toward a house on the corner.

Joe gave one lantern to Beth. They both followed the dog on foot.

Beth explained to Joe that she was immune from diphtheria. "Stay back a safe distance when we come to a house," Beth said as they walked. "I'll do the talking."

Joe nodded his agreement.

They approached the first house.

"Be sure to ask Mrs. Rynning if she needs milk," Joe said.

Beth knocked on the door of the house. It was larger than the smaller cabin-like buildings, but the ceilings were just as low.

A woman opened the door. She was wearing

a knit cap and two thick wool sweaters. A very young baby swaddled in an animal pelt lay in her arms.

"I have a message from Dr. Welch," Beth said. "There's an outbreak of diphtheria in Nome. Stay away from everyone. If anyone is sick, write a *Q* on a piece of paper. Then tape it to your door. That means 'quarantine.' "

Beth looked back at Joe. "Oh, and Joe wants to know if you need milk."

The woman peered into the growing darkness. She shouted to Joe in a hoarse voice: "I'll put the pail out with the forty cents. I just need one gallon."

The woman shut the door quickly. Then, it suddenly opened again. She set the pail and the coins on the wooden porch.

The baby gurgled. The woman frowned and

then turned her head and coughed away from her child.

"My husband has a sore throat and a high fever," she said. "Is he going to die?"

Beth didn't know what to say. The doctor hadn't said anything about adults choking, just children.

"Send him to the hospital," Beth said. "Dr. Welch will know what to do."

"Thank you," the woman said.

Joe and Beth then went to more than twenty houses. Beth was going to turn after the last building on Front Street. But Joe told Turk to keep going.

"There's an old warehouse up ahead," he said. "A woman is living there alone. Don't mention the milk. I tried to sell her some a couple of days ago. But she wouldn't touch it. Said she was 'lactose intolerant,' whatever that means."

Beth approached the warehouse door and knocked.

Beth heard footsteps and a woman's shout: "I knew you'd be back!"

Then the door swung open. A woman wearing a yellow scarf and a modern-looking ski jacket stood in the doorway.

"You're not Whit!" the woman said. She held what looked like a battery-powered screwdriver.

Beth peered inside the warehouse. There sat the biplane. Its engine casing was open. Tools dotted a workbench. Several LED lamps glowed, casting light on an open laptop computer.

"And you're not from 1925," Beth said.

6

Amelia

The sled arrived at a village known as the Sandpit. It was a flat, open space on a sandbar just a mile outside of Nome.

Clearsky released his sled dogs from their harnesses. The dogs rushed around, sniffing and barking in excitement. Other dogs from the village came to join them.

Patrick could "translate" the barking. But it gave him a headache. The dogs were yapping about finding some fish bones and about the smells of the village dogs. Some were saying hello to former littermates.

Clearsky built a fire out of driftwood to melt the snow. He melted snow in a metal bucket for the dogs. Storm barked, "I love my master," and then plunged her head into the bucket.

"It will be faster if we walk from house to house," Clearsky said. He put out the fire by smothering it with snow. "We just need to tell a couple of families about the outbreak. They'll spread the word tomorrow. Then we can go to the next group of igloos."

Clearsky took a small bundle off the sled and handed it to Patrick. "These are the mail and packages for the folks here. We'll go to see the chief first."

Patrick was surprised that the houses were not built from snow. The houses looked like they were made from sod and wood.

"I thought you said we were going to their 'igloos,' " Patrick said.

Clearsky laughed. "The word *igloo* just means 'house,' " he said. "Not many Eskimos live in snow houses. Most of those are built by tribes who live in Greenland or Canada."

Patrick followed Clearsky. They walked until they came to a sod house with a wooden

door. Gray smoke was wafting out of the pipe chimney on top. Just outside the house stood a row of tall, curved bones. They looked like candy canes without stripes.

Patrick guessed they were whale ribs. He didn't think a walrus or a polar bear could have bones that long.

Clearsky knocked on the door. A little boy opened it just a crack so he could peek out. Clearsky spoke the boy's native language.

Patrick could understand him with the translation earmuffs.

"Hello, Little Bear Cub," Clearsky said. "I'd like to speak with your father."

"Oh," the boy said, choking out a cough. "He's not here now. Little Bessie Stanley went to heaven. Father has gone to her family's house to help build a coffin. He wouldn't let me come."

Coffin? We're too late, Patrick thought. *The children here are already dying.*

Beth and the woman stared at each other in silence.

The woman spoke first: "Whit told me all about you. You're that girl Beth, one of his little favorites."

Beth didn't know what to think. It seemed like a nice thing for Whit to say. But the woman hadn't said it nicely at all.

Beth checked over her shoulder. Joe was standing a fair distance away and smoothing Turk's ears. He was too far away to hear about the Imagination Station.

"Well," Beth said, "Whit didn't tell me that another person would be in this Imagination Station adventure."

"Adventure?" the woman said. She laughed. "Is this all it is? An *adventure*?"

"Yes," Beth said. "My cousin Patrick and I want to help stop the diphtheria outbreak."

"How sweet!" the woman said. "I'm here to make *aviation history*!" Her face brightened and she lowered her voice to a whisper. "I think you're really here to be my *copilot*. Whit chickened out."

Beth scowled. "Not Mr. Whittaker."

The woman swept her arm to show the warehouse. "Then where is he?" she asked.

Beth remembered the snow on Whit's jacket and his frosty eyebrows. He had been here and flown in the plane. "I don't know why he left," Beth said. "But it had to be for a good reason."

"Yes! He left so *you* could come," she said. "I want to be the first woman to fly a plane above 60 degrees north latitude—maybe even reach the Arctic Circle. And *you*, another female, will be my copilot."

"Me?" Beth asked. "But I've never flown before."

"It's time you started then, isn't it?" the woman said. "I learned to fly when I was eight." She offered her hand to Beth.

Beth shook her hand with a mitten.

"I'm Amelia Darling," the woman said. "My great-grandfather was *Roy Darling*."

The name "Roy Darling" was offered up like someone famous—a president, a movie star, or someone from the Bible. But Beth had never heard of him.

"Hey, Beth!" Joe called from behind her. "There are other people we need to warn."

Beth quickly explained the quarantine rules to Amelia: "Write a large *Q* on a piece of paper if you begin to feel ill. Hang it on your door so no one will enter. If you are outside and see someone, keep your distance and warn them to stay away."

Amelia said, "That's nonsense. I'm not going to be a leper shouting 'unclean, unclean.' " She flopped her yellow scarf over her shoulder. "Besides, I'm immune to diphtheria. I don't really care about the disease or that silly serum."

"What serum?" Beth asked.

"Has Whit told you nothing?" Amelia said in answer. "Here's my advice. Don't get caught up with all the dogsled drama. All you should care about is helping me. We need to get the plane in good shape. It needs to be able to fly from Nenana to Nome so I . . . I mean *we* . . . can become famous for saving the children by bringing the antitoxin."

Joe called again for Beth to hurry.

"I'll come back tomorrow," Beth said to Amelia. "I don't want to be famous. But I'll do anything to keep kids from dying."

Plane vs. Dogsled

Patrick left the mail and parcels inside Little Bear Cub's house.

"Good . . . *cough, cough* . . . bye!" Little Bear Cub said as he shut the door.

Patrick said, "Does that young boy have diphtheria? He was coughing."

"Maybe," Clearsky said. "But there were lamps inside that burn seal oil. Little Bear might have been coughing from that smoke."

Patrick nodded. He hoped that was the case.

The Stanleys' house had a lot of footprints in front. A sled was leaning on its side against one side of the house.

Clearsky approached the door. He raised his hand to knock.

A woman suddenly pushed the small, wooden door open. She had to duck low to get outside. She was wearing the traditional Alaskan animal-skin jacket over a wool sweater. Her animal-skin fur boots came up to her knees. A knit cap made from blue and red yarn covered her head. She carried a black medical bag.

The woman frowned when she saw Patrick. "You can't go inside, young man," she said in a stern voice. "This family has three girls. One has died. Two more are sick with diphtheria. Get as far away from here as you can."

Patrick looked to Clearsky with a questioning glance.

Clearsky said, "Thank you for the warning, Nurse Morgan. But Dr. Welch asked us to come and inform the chief. We're to tell everyone who lives on the Sandpit and beyond. It will go faster if Patrick helps me."

"There's no need to tell the chief," Nurse Morgan said. "He's seen 'The Strangler' in action and knows its danger. The disease has already spread among the Eskimos. I need to go back and warn Dr. Welch just how bad it is."

Patrick pointed to the medical bag. "Do you have anything in there that will help them?"

The nurse sighed. "I've given Bessie's sisters—Mary and Dora—some of the old serum," she said. "Maybe that will help them."

"You have antitoxin?" Clearsky asked. "That's good, isn't it?"

The nurse shook her head and said, "Our

supplies are too low and too old. Dr. Welch had ordered more. But . . ."

Clearsky finished for her: "But it wasn't in the last shipment. Dr. Welch said the same thing at a meeting with the town council."

"I'm headed to visit more families outside of the Sandpit," the nurse said. "You'll accompany me to those homes. But I will go inside. Then we'll give Dr. Welch a report."

Patrick thought she seemed a bit bossy. Clearsky must have thought so too. He leaned toward Patrick and whispered, "Nurse Emily Morgan is a former Red Cross nurse. She tended hundreds of soldiers in France during the war. Now she helps the Eskimos."

Clearsky whistled and a flurry of dogs came running from all directions. Patrick pushed the sled down from the chief's house. He helped Clearsky ready the harnesses.

Clearsky said, "I'll run alongside the dogs.

Why don't you try your hand at being the musher, Patrick?"

"Nonsense," Nurse Morgan said. "I'll drive the sled."

She took the harnesses and stood on the musher's footboards.

Patrick sat on the sled, disappointed he couldn't learn to mush.

"Hike!" Nurse Morgan shouted.

The dogs yipped and yapped as the sled moved toward the next cluster of houses. Clearsky jogged behind.

Patrick didn't want to listen to the dogs with the translation device. He took it off and closed his eyes. He prayed to God, asking that Little Bear Cub, Mary, Dora, and the rest of the children would survive the epidemic.

Turk led Beth and Joe back to the cow barn.

Joe released Turk from the harness.

Beth helped Joe carry the half-full milk tote inside the barn.

A man was inside feeding the cows armfuls of hay.

Joe introduced Beth to his father, Mr. Walsh.

"We're going to our hunting cabin," Mr. Walsh said to Joe. "We'll be farther away from everyone. The risk of catching diphtheria will be lower."

"What about Belle and Clara?" Joe asked.

"I think we'll take the cows with us," Mr. Walsh said. "I can make a lean-to next to the cabin so they'll be warm enough."

Beth leaned down to hug Turk. She looked at Joe and said, "Goodbye, Joe. I hope you and your family stay well."

Beth left the barn, taking one of the lanterns and her backpack with her.

She saw a group of men heading to the hospital. She hurried toward the building. Dr. Welch and the men she'd seen earlier were entering.

She went inside and found Patrick, Clearsky, and a tall woman standing in the hallway.

"Come on," Patrick said. "The town council is having a meeting. We need to tell them what we know."

The group all gathered in Dr. Welch's office. It was filled with books, two desks, and a large filing cabinet. An oil painting of the ocean hung on one wall.

There weren't enough chairs for everyone. The grown-ups sat down. Patrick, Beth, and Clearsky stood along the back wall.

A man stood and introduced himself as

the mayor of Nome. He called the meeting to order: "Dr. Welch radio-telegraphed cities all across Alaska, asking for antitoxin. We've got an answer. Some vials are being shipped by the dogsled mail carriers. They will be in Nenana in a few days. Then it will be at least a week before the serum arrives here."

Beth remembered Amelia. She raised her hand as she did at school. The mayor nodded toward her.

"Can the vials of antitoxin be brought in by plane?" she asked. "Wouldn't that be faster than dogsleds?"

"We've considered that idea," the mayor said. "And Amelia Darling has been promoting her airplane all week. She took a successful short test flight today. But right now, the governor would rather trust the dogs instead of a plane."

"I've met Amelia," Beth said. "She may be a

little proud, but isn't she right? An airplane is faster. It could save lives."

Clearsky said, "Using an airplane isn't a bad plan in summer. But air transport in the Alaskan winter is unsafe for the pilot and very risky. Dog teams are much more reliable in these conditions."

Beth looked at Patrick. He nodded his agreement with the musher.

The mayor waved his arms. "Let's focus on what we know," he said. "What is the number of ill patients in Nome and on the Sandpit?"

The tall woman stood. Beth guessed she was about fifty years old.

The mayor nodded in the woman's direction and said, "Nurse Morgan, please tell us what you found at the Sandpit."

"Two Eskimo children have died. But my best guess is that there are at least twenty sick people. There could be more. Many

Eskimos have already fled to the outer regions."

Nurse Morgan cleared her throat. "We need to make sure that all children, and especially the Eskimo children, get the serum. In the 1918 flu pandemic, the Native Alaskans got very sick with the virus. Half the Eskimo population in Nome died. Seems their immune systems can't hold up to diseases like this."

The mayor said, "Thank you, Miss Morgan. Every effort will be made to get enough serum for everyone who needs it."

Next Dr. Welch stood and gave his report. "I added Miss Morgan's numbers to mine. I fear that we might have fifty cases on our hands."

Dr. Welch looked grave. He said, "Mr. Rynning is a schoolteacher. He came to see me at the hospital. He has a cough, high fever, and sore throat—clear symptoms of diphtheria. He may have infected the entire school."

Beth imagined her friends in Odyssey. She wouldn't want any of them to die.

"How much old serum do you have?" the mayor asked.

"Enough for about ten people, but I fear it's too old to help anyone," Dr. Welch said. "Bessie Stanley was given a shot. But the antitoxin failed her."

Silence filled the room.

The mayor ended the meeting. "We'll meet again tomorrow night at Eagle Hall," he said.

Everyone began to leave the room. Beth and Patrick headed toward the exit.

Nurse Morgan said, "Not so fast, you two!"

8

The Children's Ward

"We can use some help in the children's ward," Nurse Morgan said. "Dr. Welch says you're immune to diphtheria. Is that true?"

Patrick looked at Beth for the answer. He didn't really know what vaccinations he'd had.

"Yes," Beth said.

"I've had diphtheria before, too," Nurse Morgan said. "It takes every ounce of strength for patients to recover. But with prayer and good care, we can keep the children alive till the new serum comes."

Patrick said, "How can we help?"

Nurse Morgan led them down the hall and up a staircase to the second floor. She pushed opened some double doors.

The cousins followed her into a long room with several narrow windows.

Rows of metal, twin-sized beds were set up on each side of the room. Each bed had a little table next to it.

The room seemed as white as if it had been covered with snow. The sheets and blankets were white. The walls were white. The nurses wore white uniforms.

Patrick counted five children in the beds. Some were asleep. The ones who were awake studied him and Beth with half-closed eyes.

"We need to give the children lots of liquid," Nurse Morgan said. "But they may not want to drink because their throats are sore. Most of them seem to like soup broth."

She walked them over to a long cabinet. "Here are towels," she said. "Wipe the sweat from their brows."

She brought them white clothes. She gave a white hat and apron to Beth.

Patrick was given a white coat that buttoned down the front.

Patrick took off his jacket and fur pants. Underneath were a regular white shirt and trousers. Like Nurse Morgan, he kept his boots on.

Beth had white pants and a shirt underneath her fur outerwear. She dressed in the white apron and hat.

The cousins went around to each of the children. They read books to the patients or played pretend games with stuffed animals. Each child was offered broth.

Every hour or so someone showed up with a new quilt or toy for the kids. But it did little to cheer them.

Patrick saw Nurse Morgan take a little girl's temperature with a glass thermometer. The girl opened her mouth, and Patrick saw the inside of her mouth. It was covered with black sores.

Nurse Morgan stepped away from the girl.

Patrick whispered to her, "Is this the Black Death that we learned about in school?"

Nurse Morgan closed her eyes and shook her head. "Dear me, no," she said. "The diseases are similar though. Diphtheria and the Black Death are both caused by bacteria. That's at least one thing to be thankful for— we're not fighting that plague."

The cousins spent the rest of the evening handing tissues to kids with coughs, fetching glasses of water, and helping children to the restroom.

Several hours passed, and they were exhausted.

Well past midnight, Patrick saw Beth take off her nurse's hat and apron. Then she climbed into an empty bed. She started to snore almost immediately.

Patrick was also tired. He sang "Jesus Loves Me" to a little girl named Minnie. She closed her eyes to rest. And Patrick closed his.

Amelia Again

Somewhere in the ward, a clock chimed
eight times. Beth sat straight up in bed. *It's
morning. I must visit Amelia!* she thought.

Beth dressed in her fur parka, pants,
and boots. She grabbed the lantern and
backpack.

Patrick was still asleep in a chair next to a
little girl's bed. Beth had been too busy to tell
him about Amelia's plane the day before. She

thought about waking him, but she decided to let him sleep.

Beth told Nurse Morgan where she was going and to tell Patrick not to worry. Then she left the ward.

Outside, the winter morning was still dark. Beth knew the sun wouldn't rise for a while. The snow crunched under her feet as she headed for the edge of town.

She knocked on the door of the warehouse. The front door stayed shut. But a large plank door on the side of the building slid open. Inside, the LED lights were on. Beth could see the bright yellow biplane.

Beth was surprised that the plane now had skis attached to the wheels.

Amelia called, "I knew you'd come!"

Beth entered the warehouse and closed the door behind her.

Amelia Darling was standing next to the

airplane's wing. She wore a black bomber jacket over neoprene clothes. A bright yellow scarf that perfectly matched the airplane's color was draped around her neck.

The pilot was studying a large piece of paper that was spread out on the lower wing.

Beth approached the plane, blew out the lantern, and set it down. She saw that the paper was a map of the Alaskan territory.

"This will be our route," Amelia said. She pointed to a city on the east side of the territory. "As soon as it's light enough, you and I will fly to Nenana. That will prove we can transport the serum in just hours."

"The children of Nome are running out of time," Beth said. "It will be nearly two weeks before they get help."

"Ah! But a small miracle will happen today," Amelia said. "I read the old newspaper accounts online before I came. A small supply of antitoxin will be discovered at Anchorage. Then it will be shipped north to Nenana by train."

Beth took off her mittens and unbuttoned her parka. Then she looked at the map. Nenana was east of Nome. A good portion of the distance between the two towns was along the Yukon River.

"What happens after the serum reaches Nenana?" Beth asked.

"From there, the serum will have to be transported by sled or by plane—*my* plane," Amelia said.

"Where will we . . . I mean where will the plane land?" Beth asked. She wasn't sure she wanted to be thinking of herself and Amelia as "we."

"Here," Amelia said. She pointed to a squiggly blue line on the map. "The Nenana River is frozen solid. It will make a great runway."

Beth read the map's key and figured the distance. "How fast can the airplane go?"

Amelia smiled and patted the engine compartment. "It used to go sixty-five. But with the improvements I made, it can now go one hundred miles per hour. Faster, if the wind helps us."

"Nenana is less than five hundred miles by air," Beth said. "And we'll have about four hours of sunlight, plus two twilight hours. If we go now, we can land just before dark. Then we'll leave in the morning at daybreak. That way the sick children will have antitoxin in less than two days!"

Beth pictured the children in the hospital ward. She imagined them sitting up in their beds and laughing again.

Amelia moved away from the biplane wing and started loading supplies into the plane's cargo area: sleeping bags, tools, snowshoes, a first-aid kit, and a flare. She also packed something that looked like a television remote control with a coiled antenna.

Amelia handed Beth some goggles. Then she opened the warehouse's sliding door.

"Before we go, let's get some black-and-white photos for the newspapers!" Amelia said. She took out a digital camera from her pocket and handed it to Beth. "Press the button on the top right to take the photo."

Amelia climbed into the cockpit and posed. A smile spread across her face showing perfect white teeth. Her hands were positioned with energy, as if she had just said, "Ta-da!"

Beth snapped the photo and handed the camera back to Amelia.

Amelia climbed into the pilot's seat at the rear. "Stand in front and start the engine by spinning the propeller counterclockwise. Then climb into the front seat," she said.

Beth felt it was too late to say no. *I'm not doing this to make Amelia happy and famous,* she thought. *I'm going to save the children's lives.*

Beth took hold of a propeller blade with both hands. The curved wood felt smooth under her fingers. With all her strength, she pulled the propeller downward.

The plane's engine sputtered to life. The propeller spun round and round.

Beth dodged backward and moved around to the rear of the plane. She climbed onto the bottom wing. From there she hoisted herself into the copilot's seat.

Amelia shouted, "Get ready for the ride of your life! You'll finally know what happiness is once you're in the air!"

Beth took off her backpack and put it on the floor. She felt around for a seatbelt but realized the plane didn't have one. Then she buttoned her jacket, put on her mittens, and adjusted her flight goggles. She knew it would be cold once they were in the air. The plane had an open-air cockpit.

The round dials were built into the wooden dashboard. Some of the needles on the dials flicked back and forth. Other needles stood still. Beth didn't know what any of the dials meant.

Amelia skied the biplane out of the warehouse and down the main road.

The biplane picked up speed, and the tail lifted off the ground.

In an instant they were flying over Nome.

Beth looked down and saw the neat pattern of the streets, the crisscrossed power lines, and the black shingles on the roofs. Smoke poured out of the pipe chimneys.

She saw the hospital roof and wondered how Patrick and the sick children were doing.

Suddenly the engine sputtered and the plane jolted and dropped. Beth's stomach lifted and flopped. Then, just as quickly, the biplane flew smoothly again. Ahead of them was open wilderness covered with snow.

What will happen if we crash? she wondered. *How will anyone find us in all that white?*

Where Is Leonhard Seppala?

Patrick opened his eyes. Nurse Morgan was gently shaking his arm.

"Clearsky needs your help," she said.

"What happened?" he asked with a wide yawn.

"A message from the governor came in," she said. "Some antitoxin is being transported by dogsled on the U.S. Mail route. Clearsky is going to take food and extra dogs to meet the relay. He needs help getting it all ready. And he needs to find Leonhard Seppala, the best dog musher in Alaska."

Patrick looked at the sleeping Minnie. Her cheeks were flushed red with fever.

"Don't you need me here?" he asked. "So many children are sick."

"You've been a big help," Nurse Morgan said. "But we need that serum more."

Patrick stood and looked at the bed Beth had slept in. It was empty, and her backpack was gone.

"Where is Beth?" he asked.

"Your cousin went to meet the woman with the yellow plane," she said. "It just flew overhead."

Beth in an airplane? Patrick's eyes bulged, and his face turned pale.

"She said not to worry," the nurse said.

"Amelia and Mr. Whittaker got the plane in tip-top shape."

"Did she say where they were going?" Patrick asked.

The nurse shook her head. Just then, one of the children began coughing.

"I'll see to her," Nurse Morgan said. She gave Patrick a serious look. "You help Clearsky! Everyone is counting on those dogs."

Beth was cold.

On the ground, the temperature had been near zero degrees. In the air, it was colder. The wind made the skin on her lips and cheeks tremble.

The plane wasn't flying much higher than the tallest trees. Beth looked over the side of the airplane. She saw Amelia was heading toward the rising sun and following the Yukon River.

Amelia shouted, "This . . . is . . . glorious!" A few seconds later she shouted, "Hang on!"

Beth felt the plane swooping back and forth. Amelia was showing off her flying skills.

Beth felt her stomach turning. She thought, *I am so glad I didn't have breakfast.*

Clearsky ran alongside the dogsled for about three miles. It was packed with food and supplies. The cargo was covered by a large bearskin. Patrick stood on the sled and mushed.

"Great job!" Patrick shouted to the dogs.

They barked in response, and Patrick's earmuffs vibrated. He heard, "Good job to you, too!" and "Do I smell a reindeer?" and "Can we please eat the salmon now?"

The sled slowed at a sprawling mining operation with a sign that said "Hammon

Consolidated Gold Fields." Huge pieces of machinery and rock piles were spread out along the ground.

Clearsky shouted to Patrick, "Seppala works here. But it looks like the mine is closed for quarantine. We'll have to go to his house."

Clearsky motioned to Patrick to turn the sled.

Patrick shouted, "Haw!"

Storm immediately led the dogs to the left.

A few minutes later, the sled arrived at a log cabin. Smoke was wisping from the chimney.

Clearsky and Patrick walked to the door. Clearsky knocked.

A woman opened the door. She wore a long skirt and a brown sweater with a snowflake pattern. Short, light-brown hair peeked out beneath her gray-and-brown knit cap. Patrick thought she looked friendly.

She nodded at the visitors. "Leonhard isn't here," she said.

Clearsky asked, "When will he return?"

The woman laughed. "You may as well ask, 'When will the bluebells bloom?' "

A young girl peered around the woman's skirt. "It will be before spring, Mama," the girl said. "Daddy said he'd be gone a week."

Clearsky frowned. "Where did he go and when?"

"Tuesday last," Mrs. Seppala said. "He went to bring back another doctor."

"Why?" Patrick asked. "Dr. Welch and Nurse Morgan are seeing to all the patients."

Mrs. Seppala turned her attention to Clearsky. "A Miss Amelia Darling came here with an urgent message. She said that there would be a diphtheria outbreak. Then she said Leonhard had to fetch another doctor. Dr. Welch couldn't help all the patients."

Clearsky asked, "How far away?"

Mrs. Seppala said, "Four hundred miles."

That will take days, Patrick thought.

"Was he heading east?" Clearsky asked. His voice was hopeful.

Mrs. Seppala shook her head and said, "He was going along the coast of the Bering Sea, south."

"No one in Nome knows about another doctor coming," Clearsky said. He wiped his forehead with a mitten.

The little girl stepped forward. She looked about eight years old. Her hair coiled in light-brown ringlets. "I didn't like that woman," the girl said. "I call her Ameliaworm. Get it? A mealworm?"

"Hush, Sigrid," Mrs. Seppala said. "Go check on the dogs."

Sigrid frowned and then disappeared behind her mother.

"I know of a Roy Darling," Clearsky said. "He is a Navy pilot. But his wife is Caroline, not Amelia."

"Yes, that's the name. Roy," Mrs. Seppala said. "Amelia said she was a relative of the famous pilot Roy Darling. She said she flew all the way from Anchorage to deliver the message to Leonhard."

"I saw a yellow biplane yesterday," Patrick said.

"That's it," Mrs. Seppala said. "She and that older gentleman—Mr. Whittaker—have been working on it for weeks. I've seen them a couple of times around town. Mr. Whittaker seemed so nice. We thought that since Amelia was with him, we could believe her."

Patrick and Clearsky thanked Mrs. Seppala. They left the house and returned to the sled.

Sigrid was there giving biscuits to the dogs. She was now dressed in a parka and boots.

Patrick thought that Clearsky seemed sad. The dogs noticed, too. The dogs started to whine. They tried to come to the musher, but the harnesses stopped them.

Through the translation device, Patrick heard "It's okay, master," and "You'll feel better if you pat my head," and "Please, let me lick your face."

But it was Sigrid who asked the blunt question: "What's wrong, Mr. Clearsky?"

The musher patted her on the head. "We need your father to drive his sled team to pick up the serum," Clearsky said. "I think Amelia Darling tricked your father into leaving town."

Patrick felt fear squeeze his heart. Beth was in a plane with a woman who'd told some BIG lies.

"Can't someone else drive the route?" Patrick asked.

"Not really," Clearsky said.

Sigrid seemed to grow two inches taller. "Everyone says my dad is twice as fast as any other musher," she said. "He wins *every* race in the territory. His dogs are the best trained. He's fearless."

"Well, someone has to pick up the serum," Patrick said. "Who is the next best musher in town?"

Clearsky pointed to himself with his thumb. "This old man is."

Ruby, Alaska

The midday sun shone brightly in the sky.
Beth and Amelia had been flying for a couple
of hours. Ducking low in her seat helped cut
out the wind, but Beth was still cold. *It would
be warmer in my freezer at home*, she thought.

She had Hot Handz packets inside her
mittens. So her hands were warm, but she
could barely feel her toes and nose.

What does frostbite feel like? she wondered. She rubbed her nose to keep the circulation going.

"Prepare for landing!" Amelia shouted.

Beth sat up and looked over the side of the airplane. They were still flying along a riverbank. A small town was ahead.

The plane descended slowly. Beth felt a slight bump as the plane touched down on the frozen river. Then the plane slid along the ice for several hundred feet.

Beth had to admit that Amelia was a good pilot. The landing had been very smooth.

When the plane stopped, Beth climbed out of the cockpit and onto the lower wing.

Amelia was down on the ice first. She

shoved the camera into Beth's hands. "Take another photo!" she said.

Amelia climbed onto the top wing. She raised both fists clenched in a victory pose.

Beth snapped the picture.

Suddenly three men came from the direction of the town. They were rushing toward the plane pushing a large metal drum across the ice. Beth guessed the drum was filled with fuel.

As they approached, Beth could see they were wearing brightly colored neoprene clothing: caps, jackets, and pants. One had on an orange neoprene ski mask. Their clothes were from many years in the future.

Beth's jaw dropped in shock. "Did you pay them for the fuel with those clothes?" she asked Amelia.

"Of course," Amelia said. "I couldn't exactly wire them cash from the future. How else was I supposed to get fuel out here to Timbuktu?"

Beth looked around her. "Is this really Timbuktu?" she asked.

Amelia slapped her forehead with a black glove. "Of course not," she said. "That's just an expression. This is Ruby, Alaska. It's known locally as 'The Gem of the Yukon,' according to the internet."

"*Shh,*" Beth said. "We shouldn't talk about future inventions."

"Too late," Amelia said. "I already gave those guys some tips for developing antifreeze."

Beth scowled.

Amelia laughed. "Party pooper," she said. "You're just like Whit."

Beth said, "If I'm like Mr. Whittaker, that must mean I'm right." She folded her arms across her fur parka.

"Think of it this way," Amelia said. "Better antifreeze will help them win World War II in twenty years. This is my little way of fighting Hitler."

Beth tried to think of something to say. But she merely fumed inside.

The men refueled the biplane using the drum of fuel, several feet of hose, and a portable hand pump.

Beth climbed back into her seat. Amelia settled in the cockpit.

One of the men spun the propeller. The engine came to life. The biplane skied over the ice and quickly rose into the air.

Beth waved goodbye to the men who had helped them. One of them waved back using his yellow neoprene hat. She wondered what else Amelia had done to make this flight a success.

● ● ●

Clearsky shouted, "Hike!"

Storm led the dog team away from Nome. Clearsky had borrowed more dogs to make a total of twenty-one. They were heading toward the tiny town of Port Safety. It was about twenty-two miles east of Nome.

Patrick jogged alongside the sled for a couple of miles. Then he rode on it with the cargo. He felt the power of the additional dogs, speeding along a familiar trail toward Nome.

Storm yipped, telling the other dogs, "Master is nervous. Run, run, run! Keep him happy!" and "Follow the tracks, no going back."

They came to the spot where Patrick and Beth had met the wolf. "Wolf alert!" Storm barked. "We can take him! No wolf will stop us!"

"Hike!" Clearsky shouted.

One of the dogs barked, "Listen to Master! Run fast!"

Patrick shouted to Clearsky, "How many more miles to Port Safety?"

Storm answered. "Halfway," she barked.

"Eleven more miles?" Patrick asked.

Storm yipped, "That's funny. Dogs can't do math!"

Then all the dogs started yipping. Patrick heard it as laughter through the translation device.

Nenana

The sun was setting behind snow-covered mountains.

Amelia shouted, "Beth, help me navigate. Tell me when you see a large bridge. That's the Mears Memorial Bridge. It means we're at Nenana."

Beth's heart started beating fast. She lifted her head out of the cockpit to scan the area. Amelia was still following a frozen river.

Beth squinted, trying to see further. Everything was so bright and white. She understood why people thought dogsleds were more practical than airplanes in the winter. "No bridge yet!" she shouted.

The river curved to the right.

"Go right to follow the river," Beth shouted. "Two o'clock."

The plane gently banked.

Then she saw it. A long bridge spanned the river. Huge cement piers held up each end. The triangle-shaped metal trusses on top were large and silver colored.

"There's the bridge! We're at Nenana!"

A train track ran down the bridge's center.

"We're at the bridge!" Beth shouted. "Keep going straight and up a bit."

"I'm going under it!" Amelia shouted. "I'll land on the river."

As they approached the bridge, the plane dipped and descended to the river. The biplane touched down and slid on its skis for several hundred feet. Beth saw metal girders from the bridge pass by over their heads.

A small crowd of men and women hurried along the riverbank to greet them. When the plane stopped, Amelia climbed out. The people cheered and clapped for her.

Beth got out of the airplane too. She was relieved to see that all the people wore animal-skin clothing or wool jackets. There was not a single modern jacket in sight—except for Amelia's.

"I knew it could be done," Amelia said to the crowd. She walked up onto the shore and shook the mittens of the people. "Now, where is the person in charge of the post office?"

"The train from Anchorage pulled in minutes ago," one of the women said. "The postal inspector is at the train station transferring the mail."

Amelia's dark eyes widened in excitement. "Was the antitoxin on board?" she asked.

"Don't know," the woman said. "We didn't wait around. We wanted to see what fool was flying a plane in winter."

Amelia scowled. She leaned close to the woman. "This fool," Amelia said, "is going to make aviation history." Then she stomped off toward town.

Beth gave a nod to the woman. "Please excuse her manners," Beth said. "She's a little excited today."

Beth followed Amelia's footprints in the snow. She caught up with her inside the train station. It was a simple, wooden structure with a few benches outside.

Amelia was already talking to a tall man wearing a black fur coat and a matching fur hat.

"No, and no again," the man said to Amelia. "The governor told me to send the antitoxin by mail carrier. And the mail carriers use dogsled teams, not airplanes."

"But I can get the vaccine there in half a day," Amelia said. She used her mitten to motion toward Beth. "Sweetie, tell Inspector Wetzler we left Nome just this morning. Tell him that I'm a safe pilot."

Beth scratched her head with a mitten. She remembered Amelia showing off, turning the plane back and forth. Was that the mark of a safe pilot? On the other hand, Amelia had just performed an impressive landing.

"We did leave Nome at first light," Beth said to the inspector. "Amelia is a skilled pilot, but—"

"No 'buts,' " Amelia said. "The children there are *very* ill."

Beth thought of Minnie. Her eyes started to water with sadness. "That's true," Beth said. "I was with the children in the hospital ward yesterday." She swallowed back tears. "And they can hardly breathe. And their mouths are black with disease."

Mr. Wetzler's eyes started to water too. "It's that bad, is it?" he asked.

Beth nodded. "Every minute counts."

The man began to pace along the wooden floor. Then suddenly he said, "I've got it!"

"What?" Amelia said. "Are you going to let me have the serum?"

"You're half right!" he said. "We'll split it up. I'll send one-half with the regular mail carriers right away. And you may fly the other half to Nome tomorrow."

Amelia grabbed the inspector's arm and thanked him. "You won't regret this," she said.

"Now, if you'll excuse me," he said, "I've got to prepare the serum for shipping."

After the postal inspector was gone, Amelia squealed and hugged Beth. She said, "That was a brilliant act! How did you make yourself cry so easily?"

Beth pulled away from Amelia's grasp. "I wasn't acting," Beth said. "I really care about the children."

"Oh, right. The children," Amelia said with a small laugh. "Come on. Let's go. You can take a picture of me receiving the antitoxin."

Along the Trail

It was early afternoon, but it was already dark.

Patrick looked around Port Safety. The town was a cove. It had only a short dock and a few sod houses.

Clearsky and Patrick carried some of the supplies into a small house. Inside was a bunk bed, an iron stove, and a table.

"I had to use the chairs for firewood one

visit," the musher said. "It was too cold for me to collect wood. And there was nothing else left to burn."

"Are we staying here tonight?" Patrick asked.

Clearsky shook his head. "I normally travel twenty to thirty miles a day for the Postal Service. But tonight, we must travel as far as we can get. We're just leaving food here for the return trip. That way our sled will be lighter."

Clearsky and Patrick got back on the sled. The musher gave Patrick some dried venison to eat.

Patrick was so hungry he didn't mind chewing the deer meat. It was tough and salty.

The dogs seemed envious of his meal. Patrick heard one of them bark, "Every day we get salmon. Just once I'd like to try that jerky."

Storm said, "Quit whining like a pup!"

The sled set out for a place called Solomon.

There was a little light from the northern lights to guide their way. But it didn't last long.

Clearsky was depending on the dogs to know the way.

At Solomon, Clearsky stopped at another sod house. It had a large stack of firewood outside. Inside were a stove, a bookshelf, lanterns, and a few bunks for travelers and their dogs. The musher checked to make sure everything was in order. Then he lit the stove.

"My hands are cold," Clearsky said. He took off his mittens and held his palms to the fire. "I need to warm up before we head out again. I'll just be a few minutes."

Patrick reached into the inner coat pocket for the Hot Handz. He felt selfish for keeping them to himself. But he stopped before giving a few to Clearsky. A feeling told him to wait. They had a fire now. Maybe they would need the Hot Handz later.

Patrick saw an iron pan hanging on the wall. He used it to melt snow for the dogs. He took the water outside. The dogs were huddled close.

The dogs' whimpers were translated through the earmuffs. Most of them were just tired and hungry. But two of them had hurt paws.

Patrick inspected those two dogs' paws. The pads were cracked. A layer of frozen blood had formed on the pads and between their toes.

Patrick went inside and told Clearsky about the injured dogs.

"I was afraid that might happen," Clearsky said. "We can put those two dogs in sacks to keep them warm. They can ride on the sled till the next stop."

The next stop was Bluff, a mining town surrounded by tall, gray bluffs.

Patrick met an old Native Alaskan woman. She had the longest hair Patrick had ever seen. The silver-white hair hung in two thick braids past her knees.

She lived in a cozy sod home with her two grandsons. They had a reindeer herd that they cared for.

The family agreed to keep six of the dogs fed and watered. Clearsky left four healthy dogs and the two injured ones with them. The dogs would be waiting for the return trip to Nome. They would be fresh and strong.

"Thanks for the dogs," the woman said. "A wolf got one of our reindeer yesterday. The dogs will help protect the herd."

Patrick and Clearsky got on the sled. They waved goodbye to the old woman and her grandsons.

Patrick was beginning to feel at peace. The moon and stars cast enough light for Patrick to see the trees. The sled glided across the snow. Patrick could hear the dogs' panting and the pads of their feet on icy patches of snow. The bells on their harnesses jingled along in the same rhythm.

Amelia and Beth spent the night at a small inn. They were assigned to the living room.

After a dinner of fish soup and biscuits, Beth curled up in a chair. She had a needlepoint pillow for her head. Three thick wool blankets covered her, but her feet were still cold.

Amelia slept on the couch with the serum next to her. The glass vials with the antitoxin were in a wooden crate, wrapped in blankets.

In the morning, Beth and Amelia put on their boots and jackets. They headed to the train station. Outside was colder than Beth had ever felt. The moisture in her nose froze.

It felt as if pins were sticking her when she crinkled her nose.

The inspector and a small group of people waited for them inside the station. "The plane has been refueled," he said. "The ice has also been chipped off the plane's skis. It's ready for takeoff."

One of the men in the train station said, "I'm a reporter. Let me get a picture of you two ladies before takeoff."

Amelia stored the box of serum in the plane's cargo hatch.

The reporter held a camera with a large flash unit on top.

Amelia posed for the photographer. The bright yellow scarf was wrapped around her neck. Beth stood next to her. Just before the camera flashed its light, Amelia moved the scarf to cover Beth's face.

"Hey," Beth said. "That was rude to hide my face."

"What?" Amelia asked, pretending to be innocent.

Beth frowned. She was about to argue when the reporter interrupted them.

"Miss Darling, there's a storm coming. Are you prepared to fly in this hostile weather?" he asked. "The temps will drop to forty below. And that's without windchill."

Amelia smiled. Her expression was smug. "I've done some upgrades to the plane," she said. "I am an expert pilot and a skilled mechanical engineer. This plane is ready for anything!"

"I hope so," Mr. Wetzler said. "If you don't deliver that serum, I could get fired."

Beth added, "And the children in Nome probably won't survive."

● ● ●

Beth and Amelia left the station and walked over the ice to the biplane at the first sign of dawn. Amelia climbed into the cockpit.

Beth spun the propeller. The engine sputtered and then died. She pulled harder on the propeller. Again the engine died. On the fifth try, the engine revved to life.

Beth shivered uncontrollably. Today was even colder than yesterday. She longed to be near a fire, sipping hot chocolate.

Amelia guided the biplane down the river, and they lifted off.

Beth looked ahead. All she could see was a cloudy horizon. The white snow and the white clouds blended together. Were they even flying right-side up? Gusts of wind rocked the plane. Snow began to fall. *We're flying directly into the storm!*

The Norton Sound

Patrick and Clearsky stopped for a rest at Golovin. It was a hilly area, and the dogs were tired from climbing. They had traveled more than sixty miles.

The two mushers and the dogs went inside a building. "Dexter's Roadhouse," Clearsky said. The roof was low enough that Clearsky had to stoop.

The roadhouse reminded Patrick of a camp

cabin. Bunk beds lined some of the walls, and a potbelly stove heated the room. The back of the roadhouse had kennel boxes for the dogs. The boxes were filled with straw.

"Remember, a good musher takes care of his dogs first," Clearsky said. "You get them water. I'll see to the salmon."

After the dogs were fed, watered, and bedded, Patrick dropped into a bunk. He pulled an animal-skin blanket over him. Storm left her box to lie at his feet.

It seemed he had just shut his eyes when he heard a "Wake up!"

Patrick opened his eyes. Clearsky was gently shaking his arm with one hand. The musher held a lantern in the other.

Patrick pushed away the thick animal-skin blanket. Storm hopped off the bunk.

Patrick yawned.

"Sorry you can't sleep in," Clearsky said.

"We had a four-hour rest. Time to get the dogs going." The musher set the lantern on the floor and walked outside the cabin. Storm followed him.

Patrick stood and yawned again. He stretched his arms. Every muscle in his body ached.

He dressed in his parka and boots. Then he slipped on the translation earmuffs.

The dogs seemed happy to be getting hitched to the sled again. "Ha! You can't catch me!" one dog said. The next dog howled, "You couldn't catch your own tail!"

A large black dog told the others, "Master puts me in the back by him because he likes me best."

Storm barked, "No, it's because you're a slowpoke!"

Patrick said, "Okay, pups, let's be nice."

The dogs answered with yips and yaps of laughter.

The gang line was soon full and tight, with Storm straining to go.

"A storm is coming," Clearsky said. "We don't want to injure any more dogs." Patrick helped the musher put fur booties on each of the dogs' paws.

"Why don't you ride with the cargo for a while?" the musher said. "Hop on. There's room for you now."

Patrick nodded. He lay down on the sled. He rolled to his side and cradled his head on a bag of food.

He closed his eyes and tuned out the dogs' barks. The wind picked up, and he shivered.

"Hike!" shouted Clearsky.

Hours rolled by. The sun rose, and Patrick saw light through his eyelids. He tried to open his eyes, but his eyelashes were frozen shut.

"Help!" Patrick shouted. "My eyes are

frozen!" He rubbed his eyes with his mittens, but the motion only stung them.

Clearsky called, "Easy," to the dogs. The sled slowed.

Next, Patrick heard Clearsky's boots crunching through the snow. The dogs' barks showed they were worried. "Young master needs help!" yipped Storm. "Let me loose!"

Suddenly Storm was on top of the sled. She licked Patrick's face, slathering it with her tongue.

Clearsky laughed. "That's happened to me before," he said. "Nothing like a good bath to unfreeze your eyelashes!"

Patrick blinked. He could see!

He pulled some deer jerky out of his pocket. He offered it to Storm as a thank-you. She gently took it from his mitten.

Patrick could now see that the sun was out,

but barely. Storm clouds were coming from the northeast.

"Where are we?" he asked Clearsky.

"Outside of Isaac's Point," the musher said. "You were asleep when we went down the steep ridge leaving Golovin."

Patrick stood on the footboards. He rode the rest of the way to Isaac's Point with teeth chattering from the cold. The storm built up more wind. He couldn't tell if it was snowing or if the wind was blowing loose snow around.

Patrick kept his head down. So did the dogs. But still they ran.

They came to Isaac's Point well after midday. It was a tiny settlement on the Norton Sound. Clearsky told the dogs to go "easy." Then he stopped the sled with the brake.

The storm's winds were at work on Norton Sound. Patrick heard deep moaning and cracking from the ice. Suddenly a piece of ice jutted upward, causing a loud snap.

The dogs became impatient. "Let's go, let's go!" Patrick heard Storm whine.

"What's going on?" Patrick asked. "The dogs want to leave."

"I'm thinking of crossing the sound," Clearsky said. "But my dogs always take the mail route on land. Traveling on ice would be new for them."

"Is it dangerous?" Patrick asked.

"Very," Clearsky said. "But it's a lot quicker. Leonhard Seppala and his dogs would cross the sound to save time. And I'm getting tired. Shorter sounds better."

Patrick got off the sled. "I'm going to check to make sure the dogs' booties are on securely." Patrick knelt next to the dogs. He checked their feet. But he also used the translation device and whispered, "Hey pups,

Master Clearsky wants to cross the ice. Have any of you crossed the sound before?"

A black dog with a white-tipped tail answered, "Master Leon took me. Ice. Ice. Ice."

"What do the other dogs need to know to cross safely?" Patrick asked.

"Follow the leader," the dog yipped. "Follow, follow, follow."

Storm howled in return. She pulled her harness toward the ice. The other dogs followed.

Clearsky said, "Seems she knows what we need to do. We have to try."

Patrick gulped. He wanted the serum to get to Nome quickly. But he also wanted to live.

Amelia landed the plane in Ruby without any problems.

Beth climbed out of the cockpit as fast as

she could. She jumped off the wing onto a pile of snow that covered the river ice.

She trudged against the wind, but the storm blew her backward.

Two men in bright-colored clothing suddenly appeared out of the blizzard. They took Beth by the arms and carried her inside a nearby building.

Amelia wasn't very far behind. She also needed help coming in from the wind. A third man carried the crate with the antitoxin.

Once inside, Amelia said to the men, "Go refuel! We need to get back to Nome today."

"Yes, ma'am," one of them said. Then all of them went outside into the blizzard.

The two flyers were alone in the small building. "You made a perfect landing," Beth said. "I couldn't see anything except snow and clouds. Did you use a GPS?"

"You mean a Global Positioning System?"

Amelia said. She pretended to be shocked at the idea. "How could I? There were no satellites in 1925."

"Well, you must have looked at some sort of map," Beth said. "There's no other way you could have landed here."

Amelia fiddled with her yellow scarf. Then she pulled a smartphone out of her jacket pocket. She showed Beth the map app. "I was just doing what needed to be done. You want those kids to get the serum, right?"

"Of course," Beth said. "But if we crash, the serum will be destroyed. That would be pointless. Why are you so determined to fly in this storm? On a clear day you can fly to the North Pole and really make aviation history."

"Okay," Amelia said. "Do you remember who the first person to fly to the Arctic Circle was?"

Beth frowned. "No," she said.

"Exactly," Amelia said. "Now tell me the names of the *dogs* who saved the children. There are books and movies made about them. There are dog statues in parks with their names."

Beth looked at her boots. "Well, Balto is the famous one because he arrived with the serum in Nome. But Togo ran some of the hardest miles."

"It's *this* event that will be remembered," Amelia said. "The governor wouldn't let my great-grandfather even try to save them. He might have made it."

"Or Roy could have died. And the children would die," Beth said.

"I want to restore our family pride," Amelia said. "I need to know if it was possible. I want to prove plane flight might have worked, even in this storm." She paused. "Whit wanted to prove it too."

Beth was silent. She could understand Mr. Whittaker wanting to experiment about aviation. But he wouldn't risk lives. And he would have recognized that airplane pilots at the time couldn't use a smartphone app for navigation.

"Why did Mr. Whittaker give up?" Beth asked.

But just then the men came back inside the building. A tall man in an orange jacket was holding the antitoxin box wrapped in blankets. He said, "I've defrosted the serum. The biplane has fuel. You're all set to take it to Nome."

The men helped Beth and Amelia walk back to the plane. The winds had calmed down somewhat. The tall man put the antitoxin in the cargo area and waved goodbye.

Beth climbed into the cockpit. *What did Whit know that Amelia is not telling me?* she wondered.

Storm

Patrick turned and shouted over his shoulder, "How much farther?" His voice was hoarse from shouting over the wind. The storm's gusts hit them like waves. The sheets of ice groaned and moved with the current.

Clearsky didn't answer. He seemed so still, like he was carved from wood. His hands were fixed to the handlebar.

Storm's nose was close to the ice. At times she suddenly turned the team at a right angle or a curve. There were large cracks in the ice of Norton Sound, but it was mostly flat and without much friction. The dogs were able to run at full speed.

Suddenly, the sled's runner caught on the edge of a slab of ice that was beginning to split apart from the other slabs. The sled began to tip over.

"No!" Patrick shouted as he jumped off the footboards to safety.

The slab of ice began to flip up. Patrick dropped flat on the ice to hang on. The sled turned on its side and slid backward, dragging the dogs with it.

Sploosh!

Phillip Clearsky fell into the icy water.

The biplane surged ahead for an hour. Then suddenly, the engine faltered, and the plane dropped. Beth lifted her head out of the cockpit.

The engine seemed to recover. Beth felt the biplane tip. It was flying almost straight up.

After a minute, the biplane soared above the clouds. The air actually felt warmer on Beth's cheeks. And she could see the sun.

She also saw ice on the wings.

After a few minutes, Amelia took the biplane back into the storm. Beth ducked again to avoid the wind.

They flew lower for about twenty minutes. The engine sputtered as if it were choking. The biplane dropped suddenly. But again, the engine recovered. Amelia took the plane above the storm a second time.

"What's going on?" Beth shouted to the pilot.

Amelia shouted back. But her voice was difficult to hear: "The air filters . . . clogging . . . ice. Warmer . . . here."

"Can you stay above the clouds?" Beth yelled. The wind whipped her words away.

"Running out . . . gas!" Amelia shouted.

Patrick rushed to the edge of the ice. "Clearsky!" he called.

A mitten appeared. Patrick grabbed it and pulled, but the mitten slipped off. Then Clearsky's hood and head broke through the surface. The man gasped for breath.

Patrick's boots slipped as he tried to drag Clearsky out of the water. He would fall in himself if he kept trying. He had to think of another way to help. There wasn't much time before Clearsky froze to death.

"I'll get the dogs," he said.

He called them, but they seemed too afraid to get close to the hole. They had pulled the sled twenty feet away.

"Storm, come!" Patrick called.

Storm barked, but her raw fear prevented Patrick from understanding the translation.

She tried to move closer to the hole, but the other dogs were backing away. Storm wasn't strong enough.

Patrick didn't know what to do.

Suddenly Storm started running, leading the dogs away from the hole.

And then they circled back. The sled whipped around in an arc and slowed near the hole.

"Grab on!" Patrick shouted to Clearsky.

Clearsky's hands grabbed on to the sled.

"Hike!" Patrick told the dogs.

This time there was enough power to pull Clearsky from the water. He lay on the ice. His breath was ragged.

"Fire," he said through chattering teeth.

"We need matches," Patrick said.

"In my parka pocket," Clearsky said. His expression was grim.

Beth felt her stomach flip. The plane was descending.

Amelia shouted, "Hang on! We're landing!"

Beth didn't understand. It was too early to land. It must be an emergency. She braced herself for a crash, hands wedged against the side of the cockpit.

But the landing was just as smooth as the others. After an initial bump, the plane skied smoothly. Then the plane suddenly jolted and spun in a flat arc. Then it stopped.

Beth hopped out of the cockpit and onto the wing.

They had landed on open ice. But the top wing had hit a tree that was bent toward the ice. The plane's fabric was torn, and the wood frame of the wing was exposed.

Beth climbed down.

Amelia got out of the cockpit and jumped down from the wing.

"Well, that was a waste of time and effort," Amelia said. "I didn't figure on snow clogging the air filters. And we used up a lot of fuel climbing up higher than the storm."

Amelia stomped over to the plane's cargo hatch. She opened it and rummaged around. Then she took the remote control with the coil on it. She punched in some buttons.

Suddenly an Imagination Station appeared. Beth recognized that it was the Model T version, which looked like an antique automobile.

"Mr. Whittaker never told us about a new remote control," Beth said. "We had one once, but it was broken."

"Well, Whit never told you because he doesn't know," Amelia said.

Beth was stunned. "You built a remote control for the Imagination Station without asking Mr. Whittaker?"

Amelia looked smug. "I don't need his permission. He loaned the Model T Imagination Station to the government. And I work for the government."

"But why did you need one?" Beth asked.

"Whit sent me home from Nome," Amelia said. "And then he shut down my project, trying to prevent the Model T from coming back here. But I returned without his knowledge. I followed your Imagination Station through the portal when you landed outside Nome. I wanted to make this flight work."

Amelia climbed into the Model T. "Are you coming?" she asked. "I'll take you back to Washington, D.C., with me."

Beth said, "The serum needs to get to Nome. Will you drop me off there?"

Amelia flipped her scarf over her shoulder. "That's not part of my mission. I was supposed to study aviation and see if I could make this flight."

Amelia pushed some buttons on her controller. The Imagination Station disappeared.

Beth went to the cargo hold and inspected the serum crate. None of the glass vials were broken. That was good. But would the antitoxin freeze before she figured out a way to get it to Nome?

She rummaged around in the cargo compartment. She had two modern sleeping bags and the backpack. She slipped Amelia's digital camera into her pocket. Then she took out the beef jerky and started to eat some. Food would help her stay warm.

She hummed a song she learned at church to ward off the fear that was slowly settling in. The groaning of the ice was eerie. It reminded her of sound effects from a science-fiction movie.

She felt all alone, but she knew God was with her.

She wasn't alone, though. Beth saw that the silvery-white face of a wolf had appeared in the trees. The wolf's slanted, gray eyes watched her. Its ear was torn and jagged.

Beth tossed the wolf a piece of jerky, far from her. "Go get it, boy," she said. But the wolf king stood still.

She grabbed a flare, but she didn't know how to set it off.

She emptied the backpack. She took out the rock salt. She tossed more jerky. But the wolf remained still, keeping one eye on her and one on a nearby piece of jerky.

Then she found the whistle. Beth blew on it—hard. She didn't hear anything.

Right, the whistle is broken, she thought. Then the wolf started to snarl.

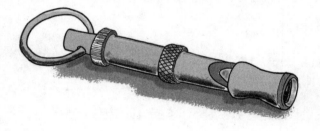

Fire

Patrick helped Clearsky stand and turn toward the sled. The old native Alaskan lay down on the cargo bed. Patrick covered him with a bearskin blanket from the sled. He took off his own mittens and put a Hot Handz in each one. Then he carefully put the mittens on Clearsky's hands.

"Thank you," Clearsky said. Then he closed his eyes. His whole body was shivering. "Storm can get you to the next roadhouse. Trust her."

Patrick shook Clearsky's shoulder. "Don't die on me," he said. "I'll find a way to get fire."

"Hold my hand and pray, then," Clearsky said. "I will hear God in this world, or I will see Him in the next one. Either way, He's watching over us."

"Are you a Christian?" Patrick asked.

Clearsky nodded. "The Christian missionaries came to the Sandpit long ago," he said. Then he closed his eyes.

Patrick held Clearsky's mitten under the bearskin blanket.

Patrick prayed quietly, asking God for help, for a way to get Clearsky warm.

Suddenly, the dogs started to howl.

Beth heard howling nearby. The sounds were coming nearer and echoed off the ice and the nearby cliffs. *More wolves!* Beth thought. She threw the backpack at the wolf and climbed onto the top wing of the airplane. She blew the whistle again.

The hairs on the wolf king's back stood up. He let out a low growl. But Beth noticed that the wolf's expression was starting to soften. His face now reminded her of a puppy. The wolf picked up a piece of beef jerky and ran away.

The sound of jingles mingled with the howls now.

"It's a dogsled!" Beth shouted. "This whistle isn't broken—it's a dog whistle that people can't hear." She blew on it again.

The howls increased.

In a moment, Storm and the dogs arrived, pulling the sled. But there was no musher!

Patrick had seen the sled vanish through the snow. "Wait!" he had shouted. "Easy!" But the dogs had been too frenzied to stop.

Now he trudged along, following sled tracks and keeping his bare hands in his pockets. The light was fading, and Patrick walked carefully and slowly. The ice seemed thick here, but he watched to make sure it could hold him.

Patrick walked for what seemed like a long time. Finally, he saw something yellow and large on the ice. *The plane!*

He came closer and then smelled smoke. He saw Beth poking a large fire with a tree branch. A crate rested near her feet. Clearsky was swaddled in a modern sleeping bag. He seemed to be leaning as close to the fire as he could get. His hands were held palms up. His parka and boots were nearby, drying out.

The dogs had been released from their harnesses. They were running around eating pieces of beef jerky.

Through the listening device, Patrick heard, "Jerky! Jerky! Find the jerky!" and "Finally, something besides salmon." One of the dogs said, "I smell a wolf. Let's get him!" Storm yipped, "Don't look for trouble, pup!"

Patrick came close to the fire and greeted Beth. She gave him a quick hug.

"I heard your story from Clearsky," she said. "How did you pull him out of the water?"

"Storm figured out how to get the dogs to help," Patrick said. "They wouldn't listen to me. Not even with the translation device."

He knelt close to the fire and held his hands up.

"How did you start the fire?" he asked.

"We had matches in the first-aid kit that

Amelia brought," she said. Then she motioned to the plane. "We used that to fuel the fire."

One of the upper wings was smashed. Some of the wood frame was missing.

Then Beth told him about Amelia and their stops in Ruby and Nenana.

Patrick scratched his head. "Where did Amelia go?"

Beth frowned. "The plane had engine problems, so she didn't care about this mission anymore. She left me with the antitoxin." Then Beth leaned toward Patrick and whispered, "She left the same way she got here."

Patrick nodded. *The Imagination Station!*

Then Beth opened the crate. Patrick looked inside and saw the glass vials.

"Is that the antitoxin?" Patrick asked.

Clearsky struggled to his feet. "Yes . . . it . . . is," he said, breathing heavily between words. "Must . . . get . . . it . . . to Nome!"

Minnie

Beth was amazed at Clearsky's toughness. The old musher had seemed near death when Beth found him on the sled. He'd sat by the fire for less than two hours, drying off and warming up. And now he was willing to travel more.

The storm died down with the setting sun. Clearsky fed the dogs more dried salmon. "A good musher always takes care of his dogs first," he said.

Afterward, Patrick hitched the dogs to the harness.

But the sled runners had ice on them that had melted and refrozen. They were not going to move easily.

Beth was worried. They needed that sled freed from the ice.

Patrick must have thought the same thing. He asked Clearsky, "Do you have an axe?"

"Of course," the musher said.

"Chopping the ice off will take too long," Beth said. "I have an idea."

Beth went to the plane and brought back the rock salt. She poured some on the ice that bound the runners. In a few minutes, the ice covering the runners had turned to slush. The sled was free.

The last thing to be packed was the serum. Beth wrapped it up in the blankets and put the whole thing inside the sleeping bag.

She silently thanked Amelia for the modern fabric. It would keep the serum from freezing and becoming useless.

Patrick and Beth loaded the sled. They helped Clearsky to the sled. His legs seemed a bit wobbly.

Clearsky stood on the footboards behind the two cousins. He gripped the handle. "Hike," he said in a weak voice.

The sled headed west toward Nome.

Beth looked back at the biplane one last time. She wondered if she would ever see Amelia Darling again.

The dogs pulled the sled with the serum into Nome eighteen hours later. The weather was clear, and the temperature rose to four degrees.

Patrick wondered how the townsfolk

knew the sled was coming. Men, women, and children stood along Front Street. They cheered as Storm led the sled into town.

Dr. Welch was at the front of the crowd. He rushed toward the sled. "Where's the serum?" the doctor asked.

Patrick and Beth each answered, "I'll show you!"

Together they hopped off the footboards and yanked the bearskin off the top of the serum. Then Patrick lifted the sleeping-bag bundle. "Where do we take it?"

"To the hospital," Dr. Welch said.

The crowd moved toward the hospital, following Patrick and Beth. Then Patrick heard the dogs barking.

A good musher always cares for his dogs first, he remembered. He didn't need a translation device to know the dogs needed water and food. He also needed to make sure

Clearsky was cared for. He'd had little sleep and might have frostbite from his fall into the icy water.

Patrick stopped and handed Beth the bundle. "I've got to check on the dogs for Clearsky," he said. "You take the antitoxin to the hospital. I'll be there soon."

Beth nodded. "Hurry," she said.

Patrick went back to the sled. The crowd had gone to the hospital following the serum.

Clearsky was leaning over the handlebar of the sled.

"Let's get you inside near a fire," Patrick said. "I'll take care of the dogs after that."

Clearsky nodded and forced a weak smile.

Patrick let the tired musher lean on him. They walked to the roadhouse. Inside, Clearsky lay down on a bunk.

Patrick started a fire in the stove. Then he went back to free the dogs from the harness.

He unhooked the dogs. Then he hugged Storm and smoothed her ears.

Storm yipped. Through the translation device Patrick heard, "Please come with us again sometime."

He rubbed her head. "You're just being nice because you want more beef jerky," he said.

Through his translation earmuffs, Patrick heard the dogs howling with laughter.

Beth and Dr. Welch carefully carried the antitoxin bundle to his office.

The doctor slipped the crate out of the sleeping bag and set it on his desk. He didn't say anything about the modern fabric. He was focused on the serum. Then he gathered some tools. He took a small pair of metal tongs in his right hand. He carefully lifted one of the glass vials with the tongs.

"Will you please move the Bunsen burner closer?" he asked Beth.

Beth reached across the doctor's desk and positioned the burner. It was a candlestick-shaped metal tube.

Beth turned a knob on the burner. A steady, bluish-yellow flame glowed from its tip.

Dr. Welch warmed the vial over the small flame.

"We have to be careful not to get it too hot," he said. "I hope it didn't get too cold."

"It has to work, or at least ten children will die soon." The voice came from the door.

Beth looked up to see Nurse Morgan in the doorway. She was wringing her hands.

Dr. Welch lifted the glass vial toward the nurse. "Take this," he said. "It's ready."

"There should be enough antitoxin for fifteen children," Beth said. "Will Minnie get some?"

Tears of joy escaped from Nurse Morgan's eyes. She offered a tentative smile and nodded. "Minnie is the worst," she said. "I'll give her the first dose right now. We've been praying for two days straight for this miracle serum."

Patrick and Beth stayed to help Nurse Morgan for several days.

Patrick saw improvement in the children—especially Minnie. The serum was working. Her coughs were softer. Her temperature dropped below one hundred degrees. He sang her to sleep with "Jesus Loves Me" that night.

A day later, Patrick and Beth stood at the hospital window. They watched as another dogsled team arrived. A crowd of people surrounded it.

"The other half of the antitoxin is here!" Patrick said.

"I bet that's the sled with Balto as the lead dog," Beth whispered. "He becomes kind of famous."

"Let's go see the team," Patrick said.

The cousins put on their parkas and boots and hurried down the stairs.

Patrick made sure he had the translation earmuffs.

Beth pushed open the hospital doors.

Suddenly, they heard a familiar hum. The Imagination Station was waiting for them outside. Its door slid open.

"Let's wait a few minutes," Patrick said. "I want to talk to Balto with the translation earmuffs."

"The machine might not be here later," Beth said.

Patrick sighed. "Okay," he said.

The cousins climbed inside. They put their seatbelts on.

Patrick pushed the red button.

The Camera

The first thing Beth noticed was the warmth of Whit's workshop. The inventor stood at a table wiping his hands with a rag.

She stepped out of the Imagination Station. Her clothes were back to her normal jeans and T-shirt. The only thing she had from the adventure was Amelia's digital camera. It was still in her pocket.

Patrick wore his regular clothes now too. He was holding the translation earmuffs.

"That was the hardest adventure I ever went on," Patrick said. "I had to ride on a sled with practically no sleep for two days. A man almost froze to death."

"What about me?" Beth said. "I almost froze solid in Amelia's airplane. She's one crazy pilot!"

Whit's eyebrows shot up. "You met Amelia Darling?"

"Met her?" Beth said. "I flew nearly seven hundred miles with her in a blizzard!"

Whit twisted his mustache. "Did the biplane make the roundtrip flight?"

"Almost," Beth said. She began to feel a little proud of their flight. "We made it from Nome to Ruby. Then Ruby to Nenana."

"Did you get the serum?"

Beth nodded. "But on the way back to Nome, the plane had some engine problems."

"I thought so," Whit said. "There was a

government mission to see if the plane trip would have worked. Amelia's mission was to use 1925 technology and make the trip. But I realized it couldn't be done. That plane was going to freeze."

"The air filters clogged with ice," Beth said. "And Amelia used modern technology—a map on her smartphone. She had other modern things like neoprene coats and antifreeze." Beth showed Whit the camera. "She left this. It has a lot of pictures of the flight."

Patrick said, "Is it her fault I didn't get to meet Balto?"

Whit put a hand on Patrick's shoulder. "I had planned for one of you to ride with Balto's sled team," he said. "The other was supposed to ride with Leonhard Seppala. His dog was a powerful leader named Togo. It seems that Amelia interfered with those plans."

Patrick was silent at first. Then he said, "I

traveled with Storm. She was smart. I also learned a lot from that brave old Alaskan mailman. That was good enough."

"That's the spirit," Whit said. "Be content with what you have."

"Amelia wasn't content," Beth said. "She wasn't happy knowing the dogsled team would save the children. She wanted to be the one to get the credit." She handed Whit the camera. "We should look at these photos!"

Whit turned the camera on and began clicking through the images. "Hmmm," he said. "She did like photos of herself."

Suddenly Whit gasped.

"What is it?" Beth asked.

"Let me see," said Patrick.

"Look at this picture," Whit said, holding out the camera. "Tell me what you see. I could be mistaken."

Patrick glanced at Whit with a confused

look on his face. "How did she take this photo?" Patrick asked under his breath.

"What?" Beth said. "Let me see!"

She leaned her head close to look at the camera's display. At first, she was confused.

"It's Ferdy, the penguin on the small island near Mactan!" Beth said. She remembered their previous adventure in which they'd met Ferdinand Magellan. Ferdy had been named after the explorer. "How did Amelia get to the Philippines?"

Whit sat down on a metal stool on wheels. He rolled it over to another worktable. Then he shuffled through some papers.

"I don't know," Whit said finally. He looked up, his kind eyes locking with Beth's. "Tell me everything you saw when Amelia left Alaska."

Beth pictured the moments after their unexpected landing. She shivered, remembering the cold. "Amelia left in a huff after the biplane's wing was destroyed," she said. "She used a remote control to summon the Model T."

"A remote control?" Whit asked.

Beth nodded. "Amelia said she built it herself. It had a coil on top. It looked like a smaller version of the coils on the Model T."

"Go on," Whit said.

Beth continued: "She asked if I wanted to go back to Washington, D.C. But I said no."

"What does the photo of Ferdy mean?" Patrick asked. "Can she go anywhere she wants?"

Whit closed his eyes for a moment. He seemed to be searching his memory. "I didn't give the government all the secrets to the Model T Imagination Station," he said. "But Amelia is as smart as they come."

"But you're smarter!" Beth said.

"Right," Patrick nodded. "I didn't meet

Amelia. But I'm sure you'll figure out how she's getting into the adventures."

Whit chuckled. "Let's hope so!" he said. "Or she'll ruin all my Imagination Station programs."

"Does that mean we can't go on an adventure till you figure it out?" Patrick asked. His tone sounded worried.

Whit raised a finger in the air. He said, "Aha! You two are going to help me figure it out!" Whit grinned and his eyes twinkled. "Are you up for another Imagination Station adventure?"

Beth said, "Maybe, but it has to be warm. And I get the translation device this time."

Patrick frowned. "I was getting used to talking to the animals," he said.

"Then I know just the place for you," Whit said. "Come back tomorrow. I'll have two translation devices ready and waiting."

Secret Word Puzzle

Dogs and mushers had to be strong and determined to make a long trip in cold weather. Christians also have to withstand hard times. On the next page, finish the puzzle by solving the numbered clues and writing in the answers in the corresponding squares. The highlighted squares will help you finish the Bible verse and find the secret word.

"Consider it a great joy, my brothers,
whenever you experience various trials,
knowing that the testing of your faith
produces _____."

—James 1:2-3 (HCSB)

___ ___ ___ ___ ___ ___ ___ ___ ___
1   2   3   4   5   6   7   8   9

Secret Word Puzzle

1. Used for transport over snow (page 19)

2. Alaskan city with a long bridge and train station (page 97)

3. A widespread outbreak of a disease (page 58)

4. Person who drives a dog sled (page 19)

5. Nurse Emily's last name (page 57)

6. Name of the area where the Native Alaskans lived (page 45)

7. Mr. Seppala's first name (page 81)

8. The doctor's last name (page 35)

9. The town where the diphtheria epidemic broke out (page 32)

Go to **TheImaginationStation.com.**
Find the cover of this book.
Click on "Secret Word."
Type in the answer,
and you'll receive a prize.

Author and Illustrator

Author **MARIANNE HERING** has been making reading fun since she joined the staff of *Focus on the Family Clubhouse* and *Club Jr.* magazines in 1987. When she isn't writing, she's adventuring in the Colorado Rockies with her family and dog, Sam. Find out more about The Imagination Station books and other fun stuff at MarianneHering.com.

Born in Brazil, illustrator **SERGIO CARIELLO** attended the Word of Life Bible Institute and the Joe Kubert School of Cartoon and Graphic Art. He's worked as an art teacher and illustrator for many publishers, including Marvel, DC Comics, Disney, David C Cook, Crossgen, and Zondervan. He's also illustrated many books for Focus on the Family, including The Imagination Station series.

To learn about the next book in this series, *Land of the Lost*, visit TheImaginationStation.com.

THE KEY TO ADVENTURE LIES WITHIN YOUR IMAGINATION.

OVER **1 MILLION** SOLD IN SERIES

COLLECT ALL OF THEM TODAY!

AVAILABLE AT A CHRISTIAN RETAILER NEAR YOU